Tawia goes to sea

Meshack Asare

Sub-Saharan Publishers

This colour edition first published in 2007 by
Sub-Saharan Publishers
P.O. BOX LG358,
LEGON, ACCRA, GHANA

© Text and Illustrations Meshack Asare 1970, 2007

ISBN: 978-9988-647-05-6

This Printing 2007

Typesetting and Graphics by Kwabena Agyepong

Tawia lives in a fishing village near Accra. It is a busy village. The men in the village go out to sea in their canoes and bring back plenty of fish for the women to sell.

3

Each Saturday when there is no school, he gets up early and helps the men carry their nets to the beach.

There, like a strong man, he will also push and turn and roll the big heavy canoes with the others. It is hard work but he always helps until the canoe gets into the water. Then as the men climb into it they say to him, "You are too young to go to sea."

5

One Saturday morning he carried some nets to the beach. They belonged to Paa Nii, his uncle. Paa Nii owned the canoe called "Water Baby" and Tawia was very happy to help the men tow it into the water. When it got into the water he said, 'Please, uncle, I want to go with you today." But his uncle said," No, Tawia. You are too young now. One day when you are as big and strong as I am, I will take you along."

6

So they rowed away, leaving him on the beach. Many canoes rowed away but not one of them took him out to sea. "You are too young to go to sea," they all said.

There were many canoes. There were those with moons and stars painted on their sides, those with fishes, those with darts and circles, and those with lizards. There were also those that had sails on them They looked like half balloons when the wind blew them. But they all went out to sea, leaving him on the beach.

Away, far , far away they went. As he looked at them from the beach, they got smaller and smaller until they looked like ants. Soon they got so small that he could not see them and he had to climb up a coconut tree.

Up in the coconut fronds, there was a dry pod that looked very much like a canoe. Tawiah began thinking of a little canoe and little men on a little sea. "Now," he thought, "I will make my own little canoe."

Soon in the shade of the coconut tree he was making his little canoe.

There were many people on the beach. Some were busy mending their nets; others were repairing their canoes. Some were hauling in their nets and others were just swimming in the sea. There were also the women who were talking to each other and waiting for the fishermen. There were the old men too, sitting together and talking about the days when they also went out to sea in canoes. There were many boys too, splashing in the water or fishing with their hooks. But nobody knew what Tawia was doing.

He worked very hard. He made his little men with twigs. Then he made their little seats in their little canoe with sticks. Then he finished his little canoe and his little men.

But where could he find a little sea? There was none he could find. It was the same mighty sea with its big, white waves.

15

"So what?" he asked himself. "Perhaps if I put it in the sea, it will carry it away like a big canoe with big people in it."

But as he was putting it in the water, a big white wave poured its water on him with a mighty splash! "Oops," he said to himself, "my little canoe is gone!"

Wiping his face, he began to look for his canoe. He looked left and then right but it was not there! Then he looked in front of him in the water, but there was only one twigman bobbing up and down. Quickly, he took him in his hand and turned.

18

"There it is!" he shouted. The canoe was lying
on the sands with the men scattered around it.
He collected them and arranged them again.
Then as if he was talking to real men, he said,
"Now we will watch out for the waves"

19

He waded in the water and set the little coconut canoe and the twigmen in the water. Then the ripples of the water carried the coconut canoe up and down. How he wished he were also a twigman! As the canoe danced, he beat the water and shouted happily, "My canoe is gone! My canoe is gone!"

One of the men said, "Look over there. A little boy is in trouble."

Hearing the little boy and seeing splashes, everybody ran towards the water. The men mending their nets left their nets and ran. Those repairing the canoes left the canoes and ran.

The old men stopped talking to one another and limped. Women picked up their babies and rushed. Boys left their fishing lines and dashed, all towards Tawia. "He is in trouble" they thought.

As the people came closer, Tawia pointed to the little canoe with the little men and happily shouted, "There goes my canoe!" Some of the men came right into the water where Tawia was standing.

Just then the men who had gone to sea started to come back in their canoes. "Water Baby" also came. As soon as the fishermen had pushed it out of the water, Uncle Paa Nii ran to the people who had gathered around Tawia. "What's the meaning of all this? Why are the people watching Tawia?" he asked.

When he got there, he saw the little canoe and asked, "Whose is it? Who made it." The people answered, "It was made by Tawia". "Hey , Tawia!" Uncle Paa Nii shouted happily, "You are a clever boy. I will take you out to sea next time!"

26

When the time came, Tawia sat in the canoe and watched his uncle
and the men row.

When he looked back, he did not see the houses and the tall coconut trees. All he saw was a grey line across the horizon like the back of a crocodile. Later, there was nothing at all but water. They dropped the anchor and cast the nets. What hard work it was to draw in the nets!

Back on the beach, they pushed the canoe onto the sands.

The women rushed to the beach and gathered around the canoe to buy some fish.

30

But happily, Tawia took some of the big fish, strung them on a string and carried them on his back. They were heavy and they danced on his back. But he did not mind. He wanted everyone to see what a great fisherman he was!

That evening Tawia thought about nothing but his wonderful ride in "Water Baby", far, far out to sea.